The Coat

Julie Hunt · Ron Brooks

ALLEN&UNWIN
SYDNEY · MELBOURNE · AUCKLAND · LONDON

$\mathcal{T}$he coat stood in a paddock at the
end of a row of strawberries.
It was buttoned up tight
and stuffed full of straw
and it was angry.

'What a waste of me!' it yelled to the sun
and the sky and the crows and the paddock.
'What an unbelievable waste!'

Then it fell silent because someone
was walking along the road nearby.
'Ah!' it sighed, and a gust of wind filled
one of the sleeves and made
it flap, waving.

The person waved
back and the sleeve
beckoned.

The coat watched a man approach.
He was a disappointed-looking man
and when he came closer
he looked even more disappointed.

'Oh, it's only a scarecrow,' he said.

This annoyed the coat.
It puffed out its chest
and the small creatures
that lived inside made
rustling sounds.

The man blinked and
stared. He noticed it was
the sort of coat someone
important would wear.
It had a velvet collar
and a buttonhole that
looked as if it was
waiting for a flower.

There was still plenty
of wear in it.

'What a waste,' he said.

'I could do with a coat like that.'

And he pulled the straw and the creatures out

of the coat and put himself in it instead.

It was much too big but he felt

he might grow into it.

'Splendid,' said the coat. 'Splendid,' said the man, although it wasn't a word he normally used.

Together they left the row
of strawberries and headed off down the road.
'Where are we going?' the man asked.
'Big Smoke,' replied the coat. 'We have an
appointment at six o'clock.'
'Big Smoke!' said the man. 'That's a long way. We'll never make it.'
'Won't we!' replied the coat. It put out its sleeves
and the wind filled them. The coat billowed out
like the sail of a great ship.

The man was carried along.
He had never travelled so fast before.
They went over the back roads and out onto the
highway. They sailed across bridges and overpasses,
and swept through underpasses and tunnels.
It was late afternoon when they arrived
at the edge of Big Smoke.

'Now where?' the man asked breathlessly.
'Cafe Delitzia on Viva Street,' said the coat.

They arrived at the Cafe Delitzia just as the sun was setting.

A doorman stood at the entrance.

'Please go straight in,' he said. 'Your table is ready!'

The man sat down and ordered food he'd never heard of.

He had Tango Zest and Rare Glissando. He had Fresh Duet, Wild Solo and a grand finale of Bass Magnifico.

'Splendid,' he said at the end of the meal. 'But how are we going to pay?'

'Pay?' said the coat in a booming voice. 'We don't pay. We are here to perform!'

At this the people at the other tables fell silent and listened.

'Perform?' whispered the man.

'He's a ventriloquist,' someone said.

'No I'm not,' the man replied.

'Yes you are,' said the coat, and everyone laughed.

'Let the show begin!' the coat announced.
'I'm no performer,' said the man.
'Yes you are,' said the coat.
Everyone laughed again.

'Where are my things?'
the coat demanded.

One of the waiters took down
an old accordion and a pair
of white gloves that were
hanging on the wall.

'Oh no,' said the man.
'Really, I can't play.'
'Yes you can,'
said the coat.

The man put on the gloves.
He had never played before, but the coat
and the gloves knew all the notes.
The big sleeves worked the
bellows and the fingers of the
gloves flew across the keys
in a white blur.

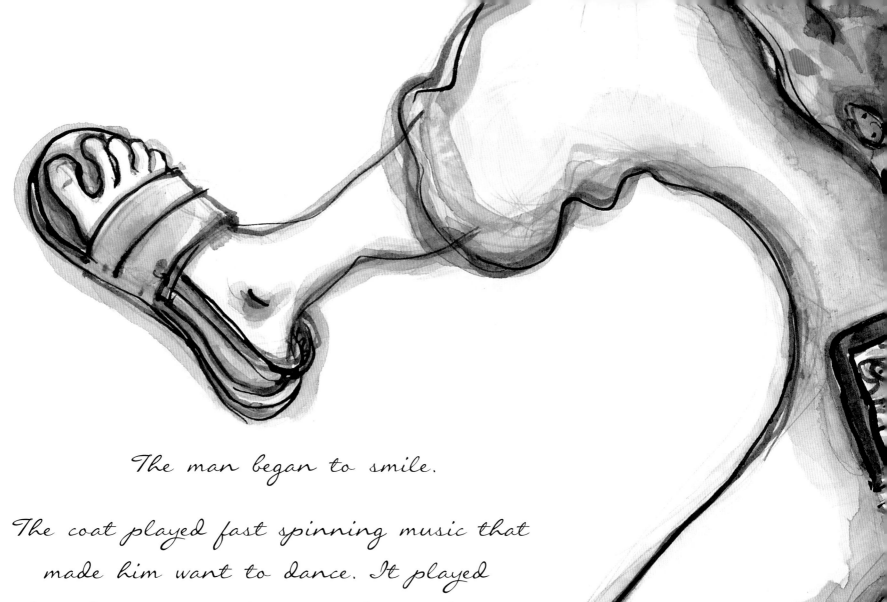

The man began to smile.

The coat played fast spinning music that
made him want to dance. It played
heartbreaking gipsy tunes that made
tears stand in his eyes. It played
crazy circus music that turned
him upside down.

The man started to sing.

His voice was thin at first
but then it grew and so did he.

The man sang a wild, twirling song that made the guests leap onto the tables and dance among the crockery.

He sang a long, sad song that made
the audience lie on the floor and weep.

He sang high-flying
songs that turned the guests
into acrobats.

All night the coat
played and the man sang.
By the end of the performance
the coat fitted him
perfectly.

The audience went wild.

'Bravo,' they cried. 'Bravo. Bravo!'

'Thank you,' cried the coat.

'Thank you,' said the man.

The man and the coat took a final bow
and walked out of the Cafe Delitzia
to thunderous applause.

'Where are you going?' the doorman asked.
'When will you be back?'
'Who knows,' said the man.
'Who knows,' said the coat.

And they strode off into the night.

To MFC Terry Plane, and to John Z and the boys, Fisitalia and Scandalli. JH
For Julie — for the story, and for her patience. RB

This project has been assisted by the Australian Government through the Australia Council,
its arts funding and advisory body.

First published in 2012

Allen & Unwin
83 Alexander Street
Crows Nest NSW 2065
Australia
Phone: (61 2) 8425 0100
Fax: (61 2) 9906 2218
Email: info@allenandunwin.com
Web: www.allenandunwin.com

A Cataloguing-in-Publication entry is available
from the National Library of Australia
www.trove.nla.gov.au

ISBN 978 1 74114 605 9

Teachers' notes available from www.allenandunwin.com

Artwork: Reed pen, brush, ink and shellac, on watercolour paper

Designed by Ron Brooks
Type design and setting by Sandra Nobes
Text set in 26 pt Callie Hand by Sandra Nobes
Colour reproduction by Splitting Image, Clayton, Victoria
This book was printed in April 2013 through Asia Pacific Offset Limited,
Flat A & B, 7/F Yeung Yiu Chung (NO.8) Industrial Building, 20 Wang Hoi Road,
Kowloon Bay, Hong Kong
3 5 7 9 10 8 6 4 2

princet⬡n

Princeton Public Library
Princeton, New Jersey
www.princetonlibrary.org
609.924.9529